Mary Frank Library
P-H-M School Corporation
Granger, IN 46530

W9-AFZ-555

MARY FRANK SCHOOL LIBRARY

T 7545

E
Gra   Graham, Amanda

       Who Wants Arthur?

DEMCO

WHO WANTS
Arthur?

Library of Congress Cataloging-in-Publication Data

Graham, Amanda, 1961-
  Who wants Arthur?

  (A Quality time book)
  Rev. ed. of: Who Wants Arthur
  Summary: Arthur, a dog in a pet store waiting to be
adopted, takes on the identities of other animals he
thinks might be more appealing, until discovering that
he can be a success as himself.
  [1. Dogs—Fiction. 2. Pets—Fiction. 3. Individual-
ity—Fiction] I. Gynell, Donna, ill. II. Graham,
Amanda, 1961-   . Arthur. III. Title.
PZ7.G75166Wh 1987 [E]   88-42959
ISBN 1-55532-868-7 (lib. bdg.)
ISBN 1-55532-893-8 (Big Book)
ISBN 1-55532-943-8 (Soft-cover)

North American edition first published in 1987 by

Gareth Stevens, Inc.
7317 West Green Tree Road
Milwaukee, WI 53223, USA

Text copyright © 1984 by Amanda Graham
Illustrations copyright © 1984 by Donna Gynell

All rights reserved. No part of this book may be reproduced or used
in any form or by any means without permission in writing from Gareth Stevens, Inc.

First published in Australia as *Arthur* by ERA Publications.

1 2 3 4 5 6 7 8 9 93 92 91 90 89 88

WHO WANTS
Arthur?

Story by Amanda Graham   Pictures by Donna Gynell

Gareth Stevens Publishing

Milwaukee

Arthur was a very ordinary dog.

He lived in Mrs. Humber's Pet Shop
with many other animals.
But Arthur was the only dog.
All the other dogs had been sold
because dogs were very popular —
all the dogs except Arthur.

He was just an ordinary brown dog,
who dearly wanted a home,
with a pair of old slippers to chew.

On Monday morning,
Mrs. Humber put some rabbits
in the window.

By the end of the day,
the window was empty —
except for Arthur.

Nobody wanted an ordinary brown dog.
Everybody wanted rabbits.

So that night,
when all was quiet,
Arthur practiced being a rabbit.

He practiced eating carrots
and poking out his front teeth
and making his ears stand up straight.

He practiced very hard
until he was sure
he could be a rabbit.

The next morning,
Mrs. Humber put some snakes in the window.

By the end of the day,
the window was empty —
except for Arthur.

Nobody wanted an ordinary brown dog,
not even one who acted like a rabbit.
Everybody wanted snakes.

So that night,
when all was quiet,
Arthur practiced being a snake.

He practiced

h i s s i n g

and *slithering*

and sl$_i$d$_i$n$_g$

and looking c^{o}ol.

He practiced very hard,
until he was sure
he could be a snake.

The next morning,
Mrs. Humber put some fish in the window.

By the end of the day,
the window was empty —
except for Arthur.

Nobody wanted an ordinary brown dog,
not even one who acted
like a rabbit
and a snake.
Everybody wanted a fish.

So that night,
when all was quiet,
Arthur practiced being a fish.

He practiced swimming
and blowing bubbles
and breathing underwater.

He practiced very hard,
until he was sure
he could be a fish.

The next morning,
Mrs. Humber put some cats in the window.

By the end of the day,
the window was empty —
except for Arthur.

Nobody wanted an ordinary brown dog,
not even one who acted
like a rabbit
and a snake
and a fish.
Everybody wanted cats.

Arthur felt he would never find a home
with a pair of old slippers to chew.

19

The next morning,
Mrs. Humber put the rest of her pets in the window.

There were two hamsters,
a cage of mice, three canaries,
a blue parakeet, a green frog,
one sleepy lizard,
and Arthur.

Arthur jumped on lilypads,
squeaked and nibbled cheese,
purred, croaked,
and even tried to fly.

By the end of the day,
the window was empty —
except for Arthur.

23

He had collapsed,
exhausted,
in the corner of the window.

Now he was certain
he would never find a home,
whether he was
a rabbit,
a snake,
a fish,
a cat,
or a purple, spotted, three-headed donkey.

Arthur decided that he might as well
be just an ordinary brown dog.

Late that afternoon,
as Mrs. Humber
was closing the shop,
a man came in with
his granddaughter.
"Excuse me," he said.
"Melanie tells me that
you have a rather
extraordinary dog
who performs
all sorts of tricks."

"The only dog I have,"
replied Mrs. Humber,
"is Arthur."

"There he is, Grandpa,
in the window!" cried Melanie.

She rushed to pick up Arthur,
who gave her the biggest,
wettest, doggiest
lick ever.

At last!
Arthur knew he had found a home,

29

with a pair of old slippers to chew.

Mary Frank Library
P-H-M School Corporation
Granger, IN 46530

MARY FRANK SCHOOL LIBRARY

T 8733

W9-AFZ-559

E
Gip   Gipson, Morrell

        Whose Tracks Are These?

DEMCO

WHOSE TRACKS ARE THESE?

Adapted by Morrell Gipson

Story and Illustrations by
Paul Mangold

GEC GARRETT EDUCATIONAL CORPORATION

"Morris and I are going to the barn for a load of hay," said Farmer Brown one winter day. "Who wants a sleigh ride?"

"We do," said his daughter Ann and his son Steve. They hopped into the sleigh, along with their dog Spot.

"Giddyap, Morris," said Farmer Brown to his horse, and off they trotted over the bright new snow.

"Look at the tracks that Morris and the sleigh make in the snow," said Ann.

"Everything that moves on the ground makes tracks in the snow," said Steve.

"Well, of course," said Ann. "I know that. Let's look for more tracks."

But all the way to the barn the snow was smooth and clear except for the tracks they were making.

While Farmer Brown was loading the hay, Steve said, "Hey, look! I found some tracks. They look like tiny umbrellas. Come on, let's follow the tracks."

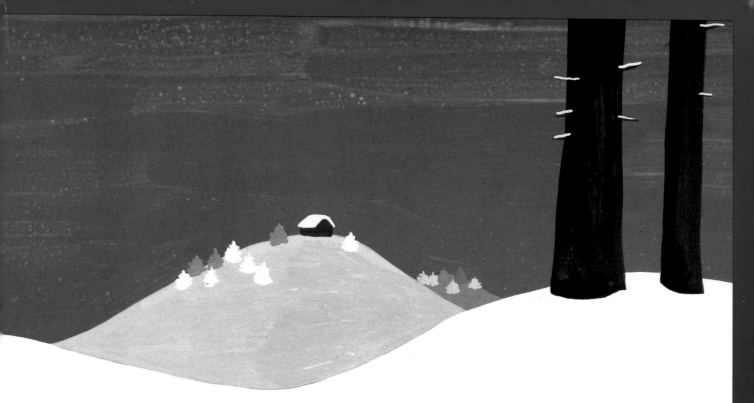

They followed the tracks down to the pond. "There's the little fellow who made the tracks," said Farmer Brown. They saw a pretty duck swimming happily in the ice-cold water.

"Oh, I know why his tracks look so funny," said Ann. "He has little webs between his toes so he can swim."

"Right you are," said Farmer Brown.

"How did you know that?" asked Steve.

"I read it in a book," said Ann.

"Well, I bet you don't know anything about these tracks," said Steve.

"S-sh," said Farmer Brown. "Be very quiet. It's an otter. He has webbed toes, too, because he swims and dives for his food. See, he's caught a fish."

They followed another set of tracks into the woods. "What's that grunting sound?" asked Ann. "Oh, my goodness, there it is!"

"It's a wild boar," said Farmer Brown. "And we must be very careful." They hid behind a tree. The wild boar grunted once more and walked away into the woods.

"Here are some big chicken tracks," said Steve.

"No, it's a wild turkey," said Farmer Brown, "and there he is. When he spreads his tailfeathers like that, it means that spring is not far away."

"These tracks look as if they have been made by two little spoons," said Ann. "And they stop at the tree."

"Yes," said Farmer Brown. "Look up in the tree for this animal. It's a marten, and it makes its home in a hole in the tree."

On the way back to the barn Steve found some
more tracks. "But they end right here in the snow," he
said.
Farmer Brown laughed, "Birds," he said, he pointed
to the top of the barn, where three crows were playing
Follow the Leader.

Morris the horse was glad to see them again, and they headed happily for home. This time Ann and Steve and Spot had a hayride. "Today we learned about seven different kinds of tracks in the snow," said Steve.

And here they are. Do you know the animals that made them?

Edited by Rebecca Stefoff

U.S.A. text copyright ©1990
by Garrett Educational Corporation.
Originally published in Austria
by Mangold Verlag under the title
NEUE SPUREN IM SCHNEE, written and illustrated
by Paul Mangold.
Copyright © 1985 by Paul Mangold

All rights reserved.
Published by Garrett Educational Corporation
130 East 13th Street, Ada, Oklahoma 74820

Manufactured in the United States of America

Library of Congress Cataloging-in-Publication Data

Gipson, Morrell, 1920-
    Whose tracks are these? / story and illustrations by Paul Mangold : adapted
by Morrell Gipson.
    p.   cm. - (Magic mountain fables)
    Translation of: Neue Spuren im Schnee.
    Summary: Two children follow various tracks in the snow and try to
identify who or what made them.
    ISBN 0-944483-93-3
    [1. Animal tracks - Fiction. 2. Snow - Fiction.] I. Mangold, Paul. Neue
Spuren im Schnee. II. Title. III. Series.
PZ7.G4394Wh   1990
[E]-dc20   90-13798
                                    CIP
                                     AC